I Know an Old Lady Who Swallowed a PIE

by **ALISON JACKSON**

Pictures by
JUDITH BYRON SCHACHNER

PUFFIN BOOKS

For Kyle and Quinn, who asked Mom to write something silly
A.J.

For Ted and Kev,
two of the greatest pie-eaters I know,
with love from your crazy sister Jude
J.B.S.

PUFFIN BOOKS
Published by the Penguin Group
Penguin Putnam Books for Young Readers, 345 Hudson Street, New York, New York 10014, U.S.A.
Penguin Books Ltd, 80 Strand, London WC2R ORL, England
Penguin Books Australia Ltd, Ringwood, Victoria, Australia
Penguin Books Canada Ltd, 10 Alcorn Avenue, Toronto, Ontario, Canada M4V 3B2
Penguin Books (N.Z.) Ltd, 182-190 Wairau Road, Auckland 10, New Zealand

Penguin Books Ltd, Registered Offices: Harmondsworth, Middlesex, England

First published in the United States of America by Dutton Children's Books,
a division of Penguin Books USA Inc., 1997
Published by Puffin Books, a division of Penguin Putnam Books for Young Readers, 2002

25 27 29 30 28 26 24

Text copyright © Alison Jackson, 1997
Illustrations copyright © Judith Byron Schachner, 1997
All rights reserved

CIP Data is available.

Puffin Books ISBN 978-0-14-056595-9
Printed in the United States of America

I know an old lady

who swallowed a pie,

A THANKSGIVING PIE, WHICH WAS REALLY TOO DRY.

PERHAPS SHE'LL DIE.

I know an old lady who swallowed **some cider**

THAT RUMBLED AND MUMBLED AND GRUMBLED INSIDE HER.

She swallowed the cider to moisten the pie,
The Thanksgiving pie, which was really too dry.

PERHAPS SHE'LL DIE.

I know an old lady who swallowed **a roll.**

JUST SWALLOWED IT WHOLE — THE ENTIRE ROLL!

She swallowed the roll to go with the cider
That rumbled and mumbled and grumbled inside her.

She swallowed the cider to moisten the pie,
The Thanksgiving pie, which was really too dry.

PERHAPS SHE'LL DIE.

I know an old lady who swallowed **a squash.**

OH MY GOSH, A FAT YELLOW SQUASH!

She swallowed the squash to go with the roll.

She swallowed the roll to go with the cider
That rumbled and mumbled and grumbled inside her.

She swallowed the cider to moisten the pie,
The Thanksgiving pie, which was really too dry.

PERHAPS SHE'LL DIE.

I know an old lady who swallowed **a salad.**

SHE WAS LOOKING QUITE PALLID FROM EATING THAT SALAD!

She swallowed the salad to go with the squash.

She swallowed the squash to go with the roll.

She swallowed the roll to go with the cider
That rumbled and mumbled and grumbled inside her.

She swallowed the cider to moisten the pie,
The Thanksgiving pie, which was really too dry.

PERHAPS SHE'LL DIE.

I know an old lady who swallowed **a turkey**.

HER FUTURE LOOKED MURKY, AFTER THAT TURKEY!

She swallowed the turkey to go with the salad.

She swallowed the salad to go with the squash.

She swallowed the squash to go with the roll.

She swallowed the roll to go with the cider
That rumbled and mumbled and grumbled inside her.

She swallowed the cider to moisten the pie,
The Thanksgiving pie, which was really too dry.

PERHAPS SHE'LL DIE.

I know an old lady who swallowed **a pot.**

I KID YOU NOT—SHE SWALLOWED A POT!

She swallowed the pot to go with the turkey.

She swallowed the turkey to go with the salad.

She swallowed the salad to go with the squash.

She swallowed the squash to go with the roll.

She swallowed the roll to go with the cider
That rumbled and mumbled and grumbled inside her.

She swallowed the cider to moisten the pie,
The Thanksgiving pie, which was really too dry.

PERHAPS SHE'LL DIE.

I know an old lady who swallowed **a cake.**

FOR GOODNESS SAKE, A TEN-LAYER CAKE!

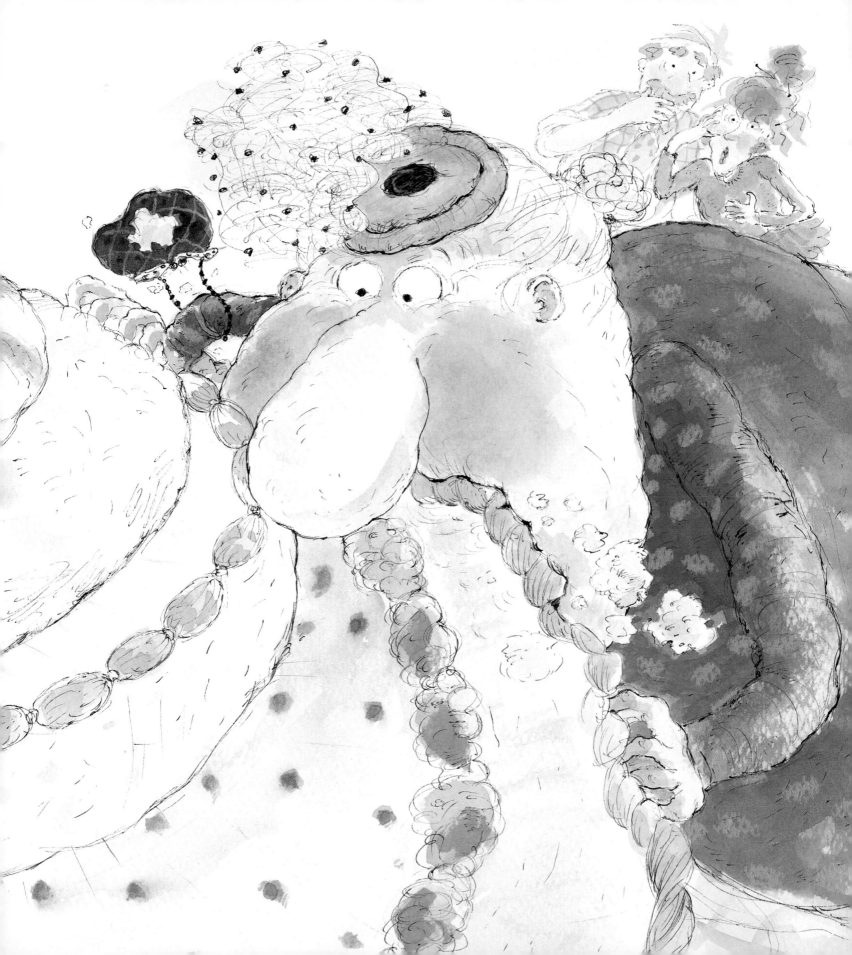

She swallowed the cake to go with the pot.

She swallowed the pot to go with the turkey.

She swallowed the turkey to go with the salad.

She swallowed the salad to go with the squash.

She swallowed the squash to go with the roll.

She swallowed the roll to go with the cider
That rumbled and mumbled and grumbled inside her.

She swallowed the cider to moisten the pie,
The Thanksgiving pie, which was really too dry.

PERHAPS SHE'LL DIE.

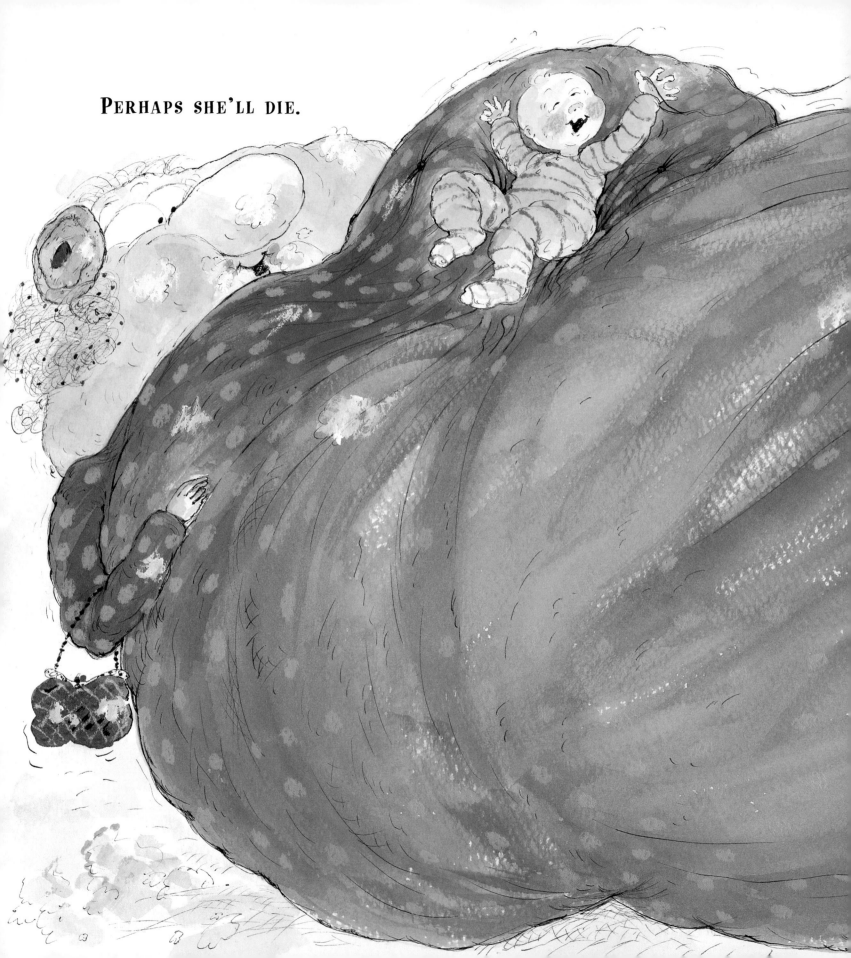

I know an old lady

who swallowed **some bread.**

"I'M FULL," SHE SAID.